WITHDRAWN

THE MONSTER
WHO ATE
DARKNESS

JOYCE DUNBAR

illustrated by JIMMY LIAO

CANDLEWICK PRESS
CAMBRIDGE, MASSACHUSETTS

Jo-Jo couldn't sleep.
He didn't like the darkness
under the bed.

He thought a monster might
be hiding there.

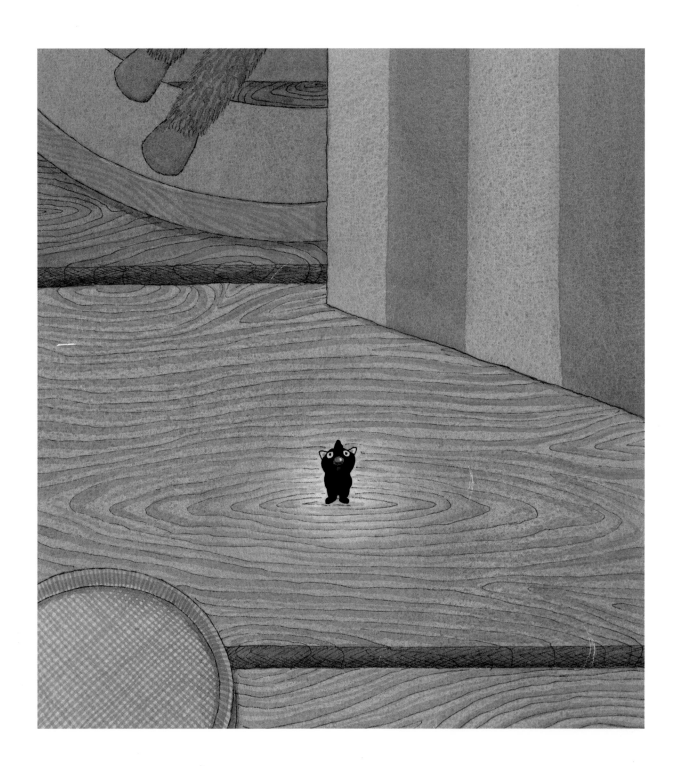

Well,
this time . . .
there WAS!

A tiny speck of a monster,
so small he could hardly be seen.

But he had a big empty feeling inside him
that made him hungry—very **HUNGRY!**

He nibbled at a woolly slipper

under the bed.

Ugh! Horrible!

He bit into a tin toy car.

Ouch!

It hurt his gums.

Then he saw
something interesting.
It was a box.

He peeped through a pinhole in the box
and saw that it was full of darkness.

He sucked the darkness out of the box—every last bit.

Delicious!

The monster was
a teeny bit bigger.
And he was
still hungry.

He looked around for
something else to eat.

There was a lot more darkness under the bed.

The monster ate all of it.

He licked into the darkest corners

until there wasn't any left.

The monster got quite a lot bigger.

But he was still hungry.

So he ate all the darkness in the closet and all
the darkness hiding behind the folds in the curtains.

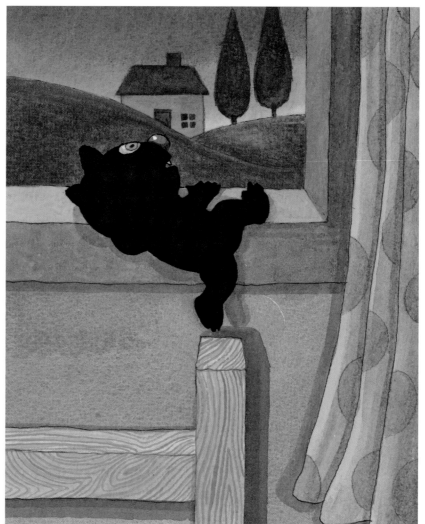

The monster
got **bigger**
and **bigger.**

But he was still hungry.
So he slipped out
of Jo-Jo's house . . .

and went looking in all the other houses

for more darkness to eat.

He found darkness in cellars.

And attics.

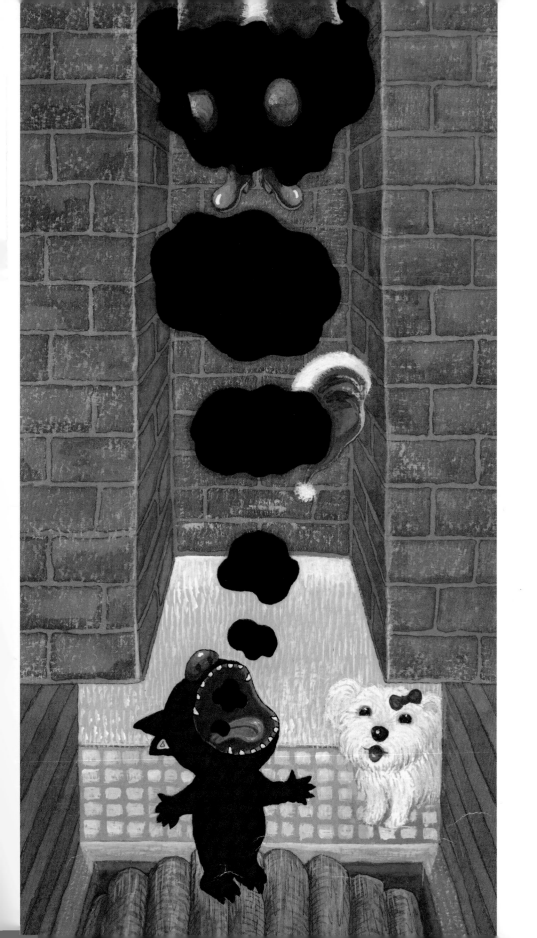

And chimneys.

He ate it all up.
He licked them
quite clean.

He found new and exciting ways to eat darkness.

He liked darkness spread on burned toast.

He liked darkness sandwiches.

He especially liked darkness soup, which he made out of the darkness at the bottom of wells. And darkness stew, which he made out of the darkness in ditches.

Then he found rabbit holes —

he ate all the darkness there . . .

and foxholes—

a real delicacy.

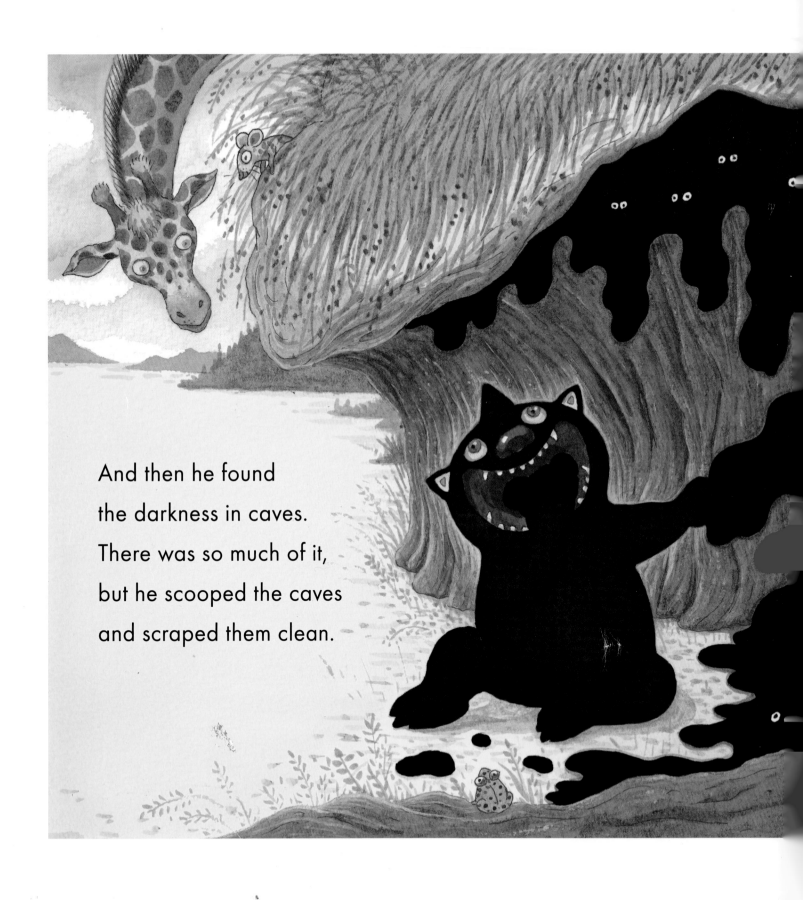

And then he found
the darkness in caves.
There was so much of it,
but he scooped the caves
and scraped them clean.

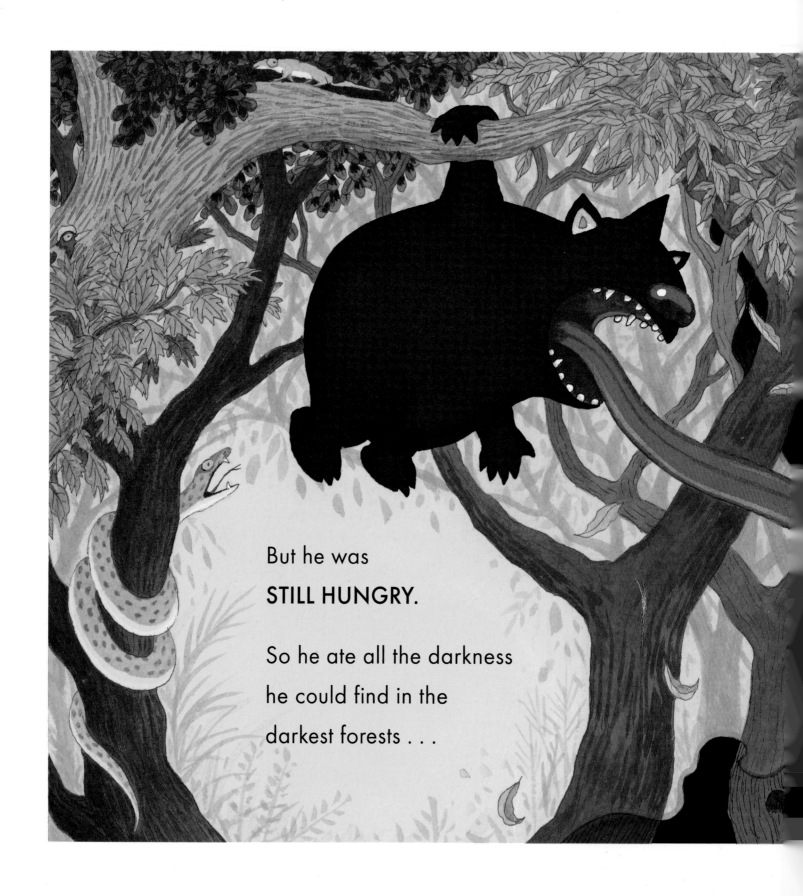

But he was

STILL HUNGRY.

So he ate all the darkness
he could find in the
darkest forests . . .

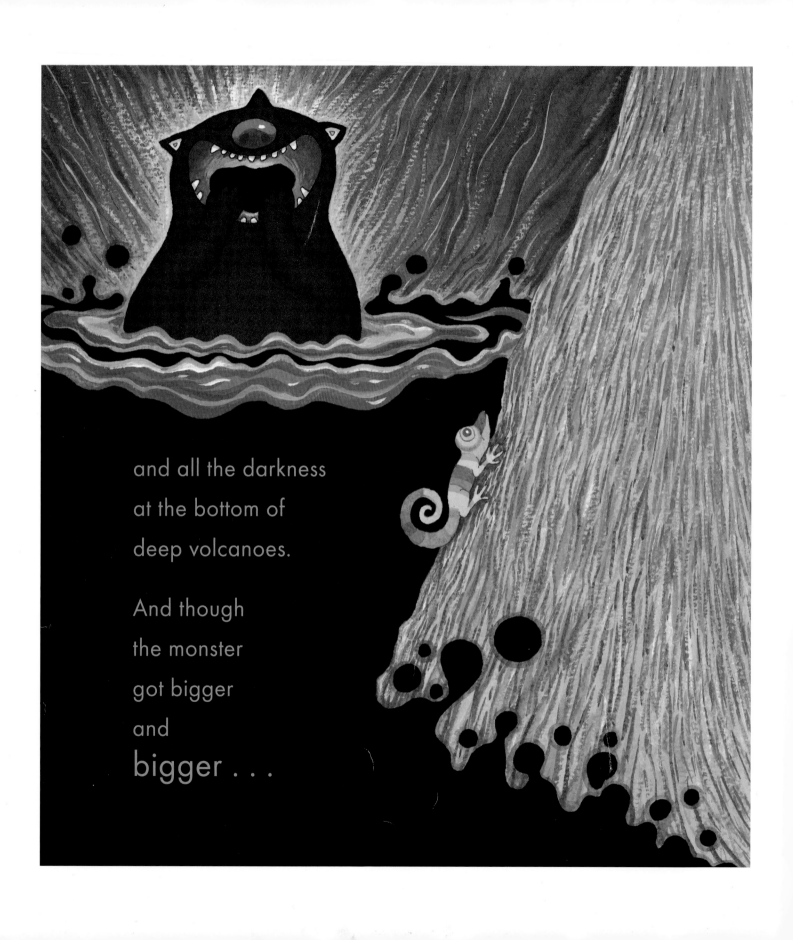

and all the darkness
at the bottom of
deep volcanoes.

And though
the monster
got bigger
and
bigger . . .

he was **STILL HUNGRY.**

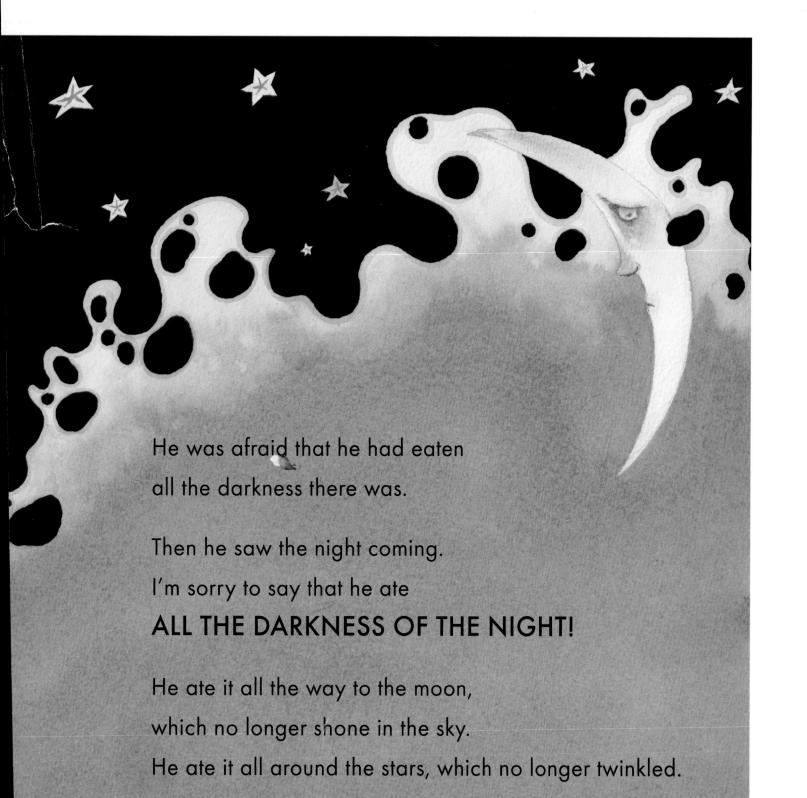

He was afraid that he had eaten
all the darkness there was.

Then he saw the night coming.
I'm sorry to say that he ate
ALL THE DARKNESS OF THE NIGHT!

He ate it all the way to the moon,
which no longer shone in the sky.
He ate it all around the stars, which no longer twinkled.

Now there was no more darkness.
There was no dawn and no dusk.
There were no shadows and
hardly any dreams.

There was only the light.
The stark and staring light.

The monster sat on a lonely planet
feeling very sad that there was no
more darkness for him to eat.
He looked at the earth.
The earth looked very sad too,
even though it was shining bright.

You see,
without the dark,
the owls didn't wake
up at night. They slept
so long and so soundly that
they kept falling from
the treetops.

Fireflies didn't bother
to go out, because
they couldn't be seen.
Cats' eyes no longer
shone, so the cats
lost a lot of
their glamour.

Hedgehogs went stumbling about blindly in the
night light and kept bumping into each other.

Foxes crashed into boulders.

Bats hung right side up
instead of upside down.

Bears were equally upset
and confused.

Then the monster heard,

from far away, a strange sound.

It was a little boy named Jo-Jo, crying.

He was crying because he couldn't get to sleep.

Why couldn't he get to sleep?

Because there was too much light.

WAAAwaAwawaAAaaa

Even though the monster was very
big and so full of darkness, he could
squeeze into the smallest spaces.
He could slide through cracks in
windows and seep through
pinholes in boxes.

So he crept back to Jo-Jo's bedroom.
He saw the little boy crying for his
mother, who didn't hear him
because she was huddled
under the covers, trying
to find some dark.

Then the monster did something amazing.

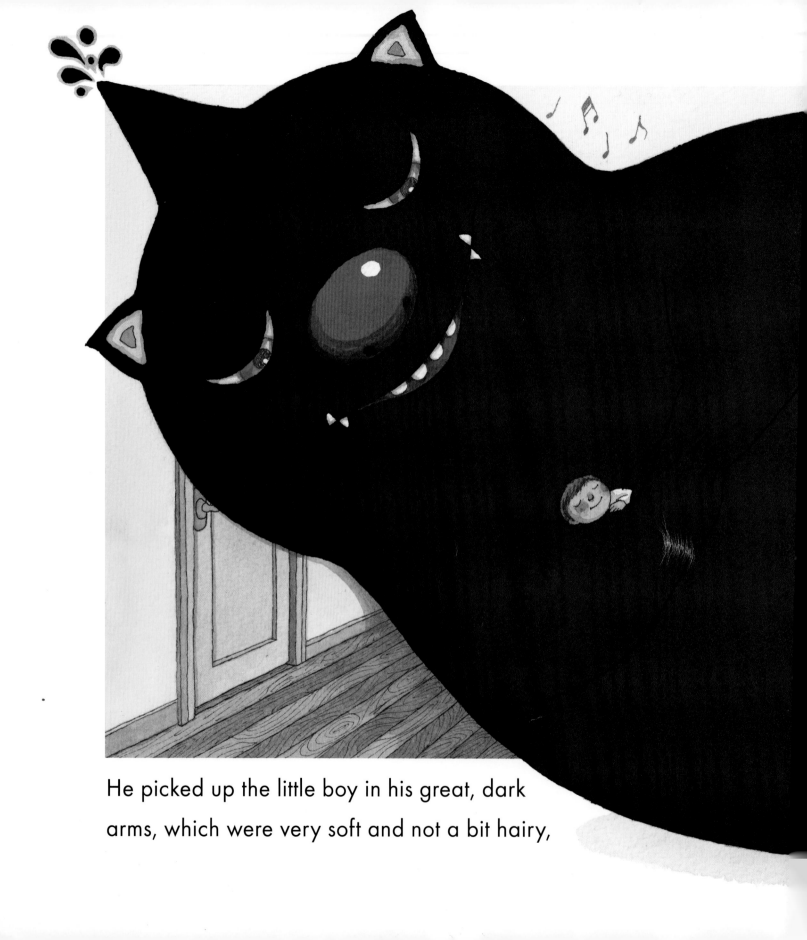

He picked up the little boy in his great, dark
arms, which were very soft and not a bit hairy,

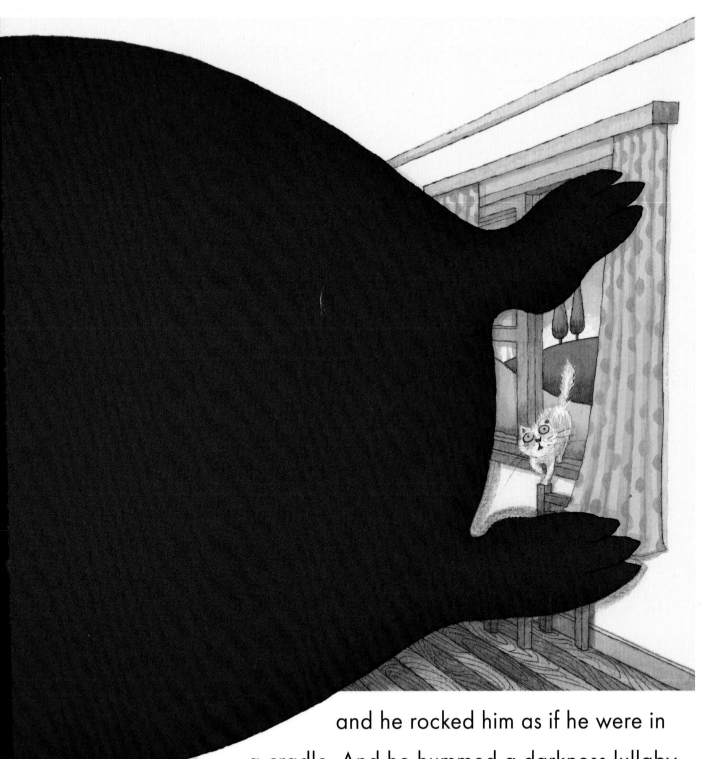

and he rocked him as if he were in a cradle. And he hummed a darkness lullaby.

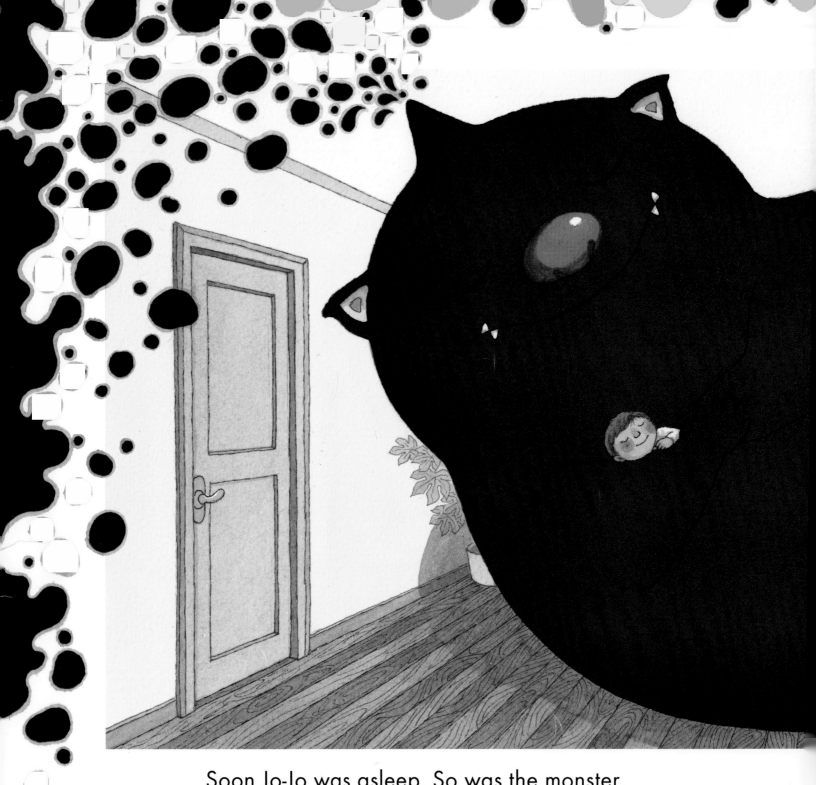

Soon Jo-Jo was asleep. So was the monster.

He wasn't hungry anymore.

He just didn't have that big empty feeling inside him.

Instead, he snored and snoozed
with the little boy safe in his arms.

And as he snoozed,
all the darkness oozed out of him.

It went right back to where it belonged.
It oozed and it oozed until the monster
was no more than a tiny speck again.

A small, happy speck,

fast asleep in the arms of a boy!

For Joe Dawes ~ *Wood Carver*
David Holgate ~ *Stone Carver*
J. D.

Text copyright © 2008 by Joyce Dunbar
Illustrations copyright © 2008 by Jimmy Liao

All rights reserved. No part of this book may be reproduced, transmitted,
or stored in an information retrieval system in any form or by any means,
graphic, electronic, or mechanical, including photocopying, taping, and
recording, without prior written permission from the publisher.

First U.S. edition 2008

Library of Congress Cataloging-in-Publication Data is available.

Library of Congress Catalog Card Number 2008928826

ISBN 978-0-7636-3859-7

2 4 6 8 10 9 7 5 3 1

Printed in China

This book was typeset in Futura T Book and Futura T Medium.
The illustrations were done in pen and watercolor with some digital infill.

Candlewick Press, 2067 Massachusetts Avenue, Cambridge, MA 02140

visit us at www.candlewick.com

3 1901 04580 9169